To Lily

For Paul,
and for Clive
for adding the parp
S.H.

First published in 2009 by Hodder Children's Books
This edition published in 2013

Hodder Children's Books,
338 Euston Road, London, NW1 3BH
Hodder Children's Books Australia,
Level 17/207 Kent Street, Sydney, NSW 2000

Text © Sue Hendra 2009
Illustrations © Liz Pichon 2009

A catalogue record of this book is
available from the British Library.

ISBN 978 1 444 91295 1

Printed in China

Hodder Children's Books is a
division of Hachette Children's Books,
an Hachette UK Company

www.hachette.co.uk

DAVE

Written by
Sue Hendra

Illustrated by
Liz Pichon

Hodder
Children's
Books

A division of Hachette Children's Books

Dave
was
BIG...

...and
quite
fantastic.

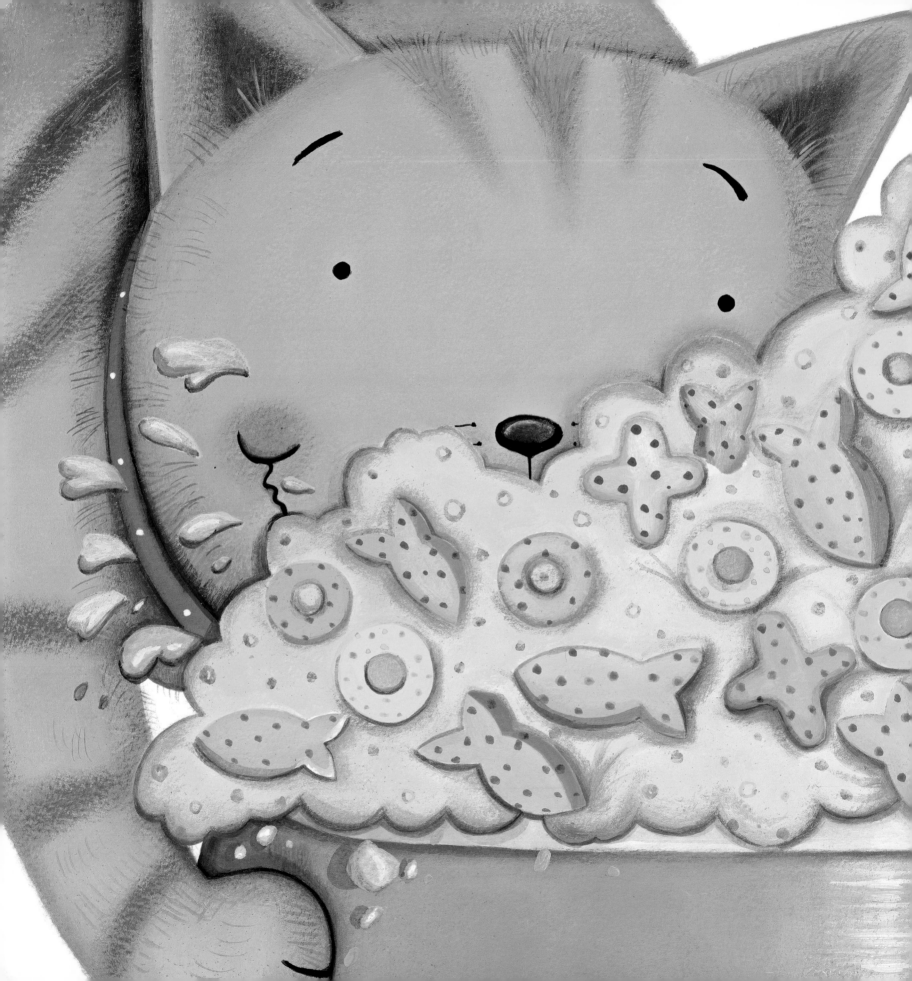

And so were his dinners!

After an enormous breakfast,
Dave headed outside for a
snooze in the sun.

He pushed his head through
the cat flap and placed one
paw in front of the other,
but he couldn't move!

Dave was...

...STUCK!

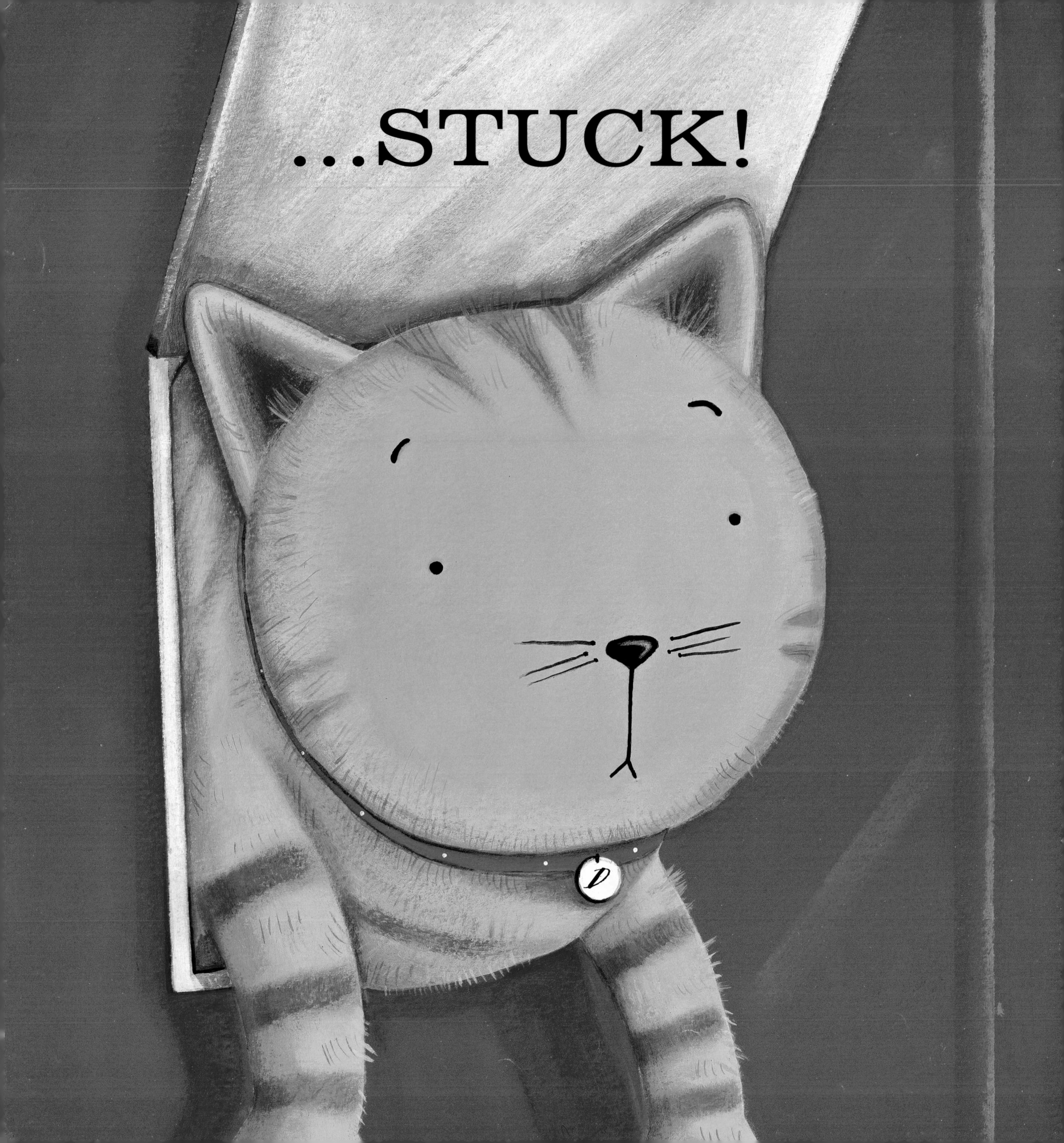

'Hi there,'
sniggered a bug.

'You'll never guess what's happened to Dave,' the bug whispered to the dog. 'He's stuck!'

The dog told the caterpillar.

The caterpillar told the birds.

The birds told the squirrels.

The squirrels told the hedgehog,

and soon
everyone
in the
garden
knew!

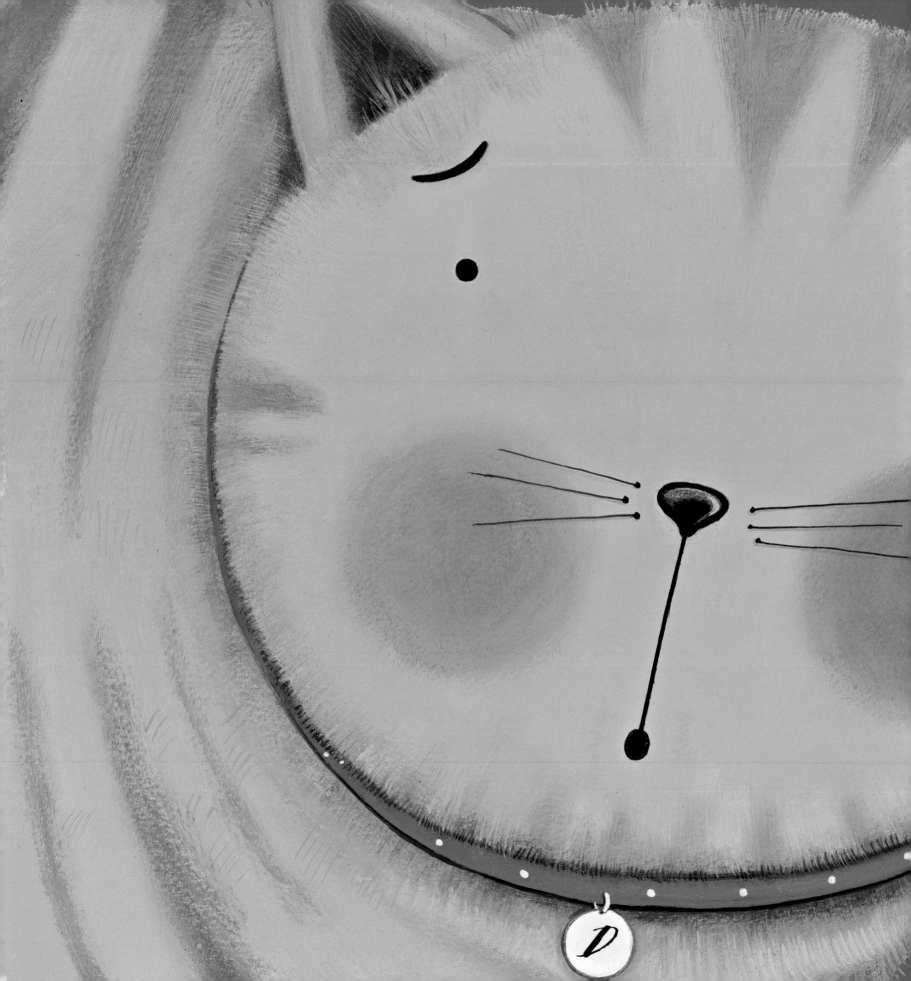

OH NO!

HOW
EMBARRASSING!

The animals got together
and decided to help
set Dave free.

Dog thought he could
scare him free.

WOOOF!

And Dave
was scared.

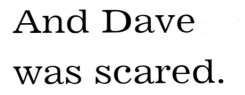

AARGH!!!

But he was also still stuck.

The animals wondered if they could tempt Dave out with tasty treats.

Yum! Yum!

Yum! Yum!

But worms were definitely
not Dave's idea of a tasty treat.

They even tried to tickle
Dave out!

Hee! Hee!

Hee! Hee!

But it was no good.
He was still stuck.

Suddenly the bug had a bright idea...

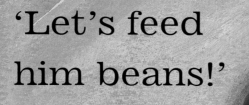

'Let's feed
him beans!'

It was a strange plan.
But Dave opened his mouth
wide as the animals catapulted
beans into it one after another.

Dave liked this game A LOT.

Dave
caught
more beans...

And
more
beans...

And
more
beans...

Until...

Dave shook. The ground shook.
Something very big was about
to happen...

5

4

3

2

1

BLAST

OFF!

It was a long walk home for Dave, but when he finally got home...

A LONG WAY TO GO →

...boy was he hungry!